So Far, So Good

So Far, So Good

by
Gil Scott-Heron

Introduction by Haki R. Madbubuti
Afterword by Dr. Joyce Joyce

THIRD WORLD PRESS
Chicago

Third World Press
Publishers since 1967
Chicago

First Edition
08 07 06 05 04 6 5 4 3

ISBN:0-88378-133-6
Library of Congress Catalog Card Number: 89-051390

Third World Press
P.O. Box 19730
Chicago, IL 60619

Cover design by Cheryl Catlin
Cover photograph by Larry Crowe

Manufactured in the United States of America

Contents

Introduction

Conscientious Wanderer: Gil Scott-Heron

By the time Gil Scott-Heron left the ripe age of 21, he had published two books, *The Vulture* a novel, and *Small Talk at 125th and Lenox*, a book of poetry, and released a recording of his poetry of the same title. Easily he was a young, young griot on the rise. His message was Black, political, historically accurate, urgent, uncompromising and mature. His was a fresh and much needed voice that hit the seventies with an anger burning bright.

His was an early genius that was able to flower and flow against great odds. Few could listen to "The Revolution Will Not Be Televised," "Whitey On The Moon," and "Who'll Pay Reparations On My Soul?" and not see that we had among us conscious continuity. Gil Scott-Heron was definitely in the tradition of Amiri Baraka, Sonia Sanchez, Larry Neal and others who brought in the powerful decade of the sixties. He had listened to and digested the works of Malcolm X, Nina Simone, Jimmy Reed and John Coltrane. In him we saw the poetic storytelling skills of Sterling Brown and the precise word usage of Margaret Walker Alexander and Gwendolyn Brooks. He possessed not only a literary soul but a musical one also. It is his combining of words with music, his compositions of wordsongs and high-rap monologues where he has had the greatest influence, making his work thunder, lightening, and wind, an excellent artistic transition for true seekers.

Gil Scott-Heron's collaborations with Brian Jackson (a master keyboard artist) are legendary. *Winter In America* and *Bridges* made serious political statements at a time when much of the Black Liberation Movement had been forced underground, imprisoned or exiled. This was still the early seventies, hot in the aftermath of the F.B.I.'s and other so-called "law" enforcement agencies' drive to disrupt and discredit serious Black struggle. Gil Scott-Heron's response was, "Peace Go With You, Brother," "H2O Gate Blues," "Your Daddy Loves You," and "We Almost Lost Detroit." You can't get any more political and serious than that.

Gil Scott-Heron in the seventies was a rising "star" with one major "problem"; he was not *mainstream* enough (i.e., not white enough). There was little, if any, fluff and nonsense in his work. He saw and experienced too much, and due to his nurturing, he refused to betray his calling. He had listened very closely to Malcolm X and read deeply into political-economy, and he understood intimately his responsibility to his own roots, music, soul. Surviving the seventies — the creative experimentations, his economic struggles to keep his groups together (musicians have to eat and pay bills too), his fighting the evil and corruption of the entertainment in-

i

dustry, family difficulties—especially with his non-prime-time music and message, was a bitch.

The eighties would not be much better. With Ronald Reagan as President, the political climate of the country reached an all-time high for the plastic but deadly right wing. Most of his records would go out of print, legal actions against pimps disguised as businessmen would deplete his resources, and the only venues in which he could make any serious money were in Europe. The eighties continued to test him in ways that affected his life and music. However, the political nature of his work would only grow and become more insightful and biting. He remains innovative and committed to the Afrikan world struggle.

His work has never lost its content: early morning runner coming quickly on the fire & wind of the sixties. strong and proactive. pace-setter and clear. like Charles Mingus and Langston Hughes taking the music and language to the upper stratosphere. groundrooted. blending words & notes with the skills of a Michael Jordan slam dunk with enough reality & truth to keep one *whitelisted* for life.

Gil Scott-Heron's own words are instructive. He wrote about 18 years ago:

> I was introduced into what is laughingly referred to as civilization. The term itself demonstrates how mankind has managed to maintain a sense of humor throughout all of history's chaos. I am a Black man dedicated to expression; expression of the joy and pride of Blackness. I consider myself neither poet, composer or musician. These are merely tools used by sensitive men to carve out a piece of beauty or truth that they hope may lead to peace and salvation.

Gil Scott-Heron is a serious Afrikan-American poet-musician. He does what all committed poets do; he examines life. His observations are recorded in poetry, prose and song. As an activist and politically conscious artist, he too is a lonely man. Few understand him, and many have taken advantage of his giving heart. To be Black, gifted, articulate and political in the United States is to be in the acute minority.

With this new and exciting book *So Far, So Good*, we enter the nineties with a fired-up and rejuvenated Gil Scott-Heron. He is now a young forerunner, having taken part in laying the ground for today's rappers and politically active musicians. They all need to go back to his work and study his innovations and mistakes. This book is an important and timely introduction to the genius of the man. After all, it was Gil Scott-Heron — long before Public Enemy (the rap group) was conceived — who said, "I have believed in my convictions/and have been convicted for my beliefs." Welcome to America.

Haki R. Madhubuti
Chicago State University, 1990

Coming From a Broken Home

I want to make this a special tribute
since i am a primary tributary and
a contributary, as it were,
to a family that contradicts the concepts,
heard the rules but wouldn't accept,
and womenfolk raised me and i was full grown
before i knew i came from a broken home.
Oh yeah!
sent to live with my Grandma down south
[wonder why they call it down if the world is round]
where my uncle was leavin'
and my grandfather had just left for heaven, they said,
and as every ologist would certainly note
i had NO STRONG MALE FIGURE! RIGHT?
But Lily Scott was absolutely not
your mail order, room service, typecast Black grandmother.
On tiptoe she might have been five foot two
and in an overcoat 110 pounds, light
and light skin 'cause she was half white
from Alabama and Georgia and Florida
and Africa.

Lily Scott claimed to have gone as far as the 3rd grade
in school herself,
put four Scotts through college
with her husband going blind.
[God rest his soul. A good man, Bob Scott]
And I'm talkin' 'bout work!
Lily worked through them teens
and them twenties
and them thirties and forties
and put four, all four of hers,
through college
and pulled and pushed and coaxed
folks all around her through and over other things.

i was moved in with her.
Temporarily.
just until things was patched.
til this was patched
and til that was patched.
until i became at
3, 4, 5, 6, 7, 8, 9 and 10
the patch
that held Lily Scott
who held me
and like them four
i became one more
And I loved her from the absolute marrow of my bones
and we was holding on.
I come from a broken home.

She could take hers and outdo yours
or take yours and outdo hers.
She may not have been in a class by herself
but it sho' didn't take long to call the roll.
She had more than the five senses
know more than books could teach
and raised everyone she touched just a little bit higher
Common sense became uncommon
and you could sense that she had it.
And all around her
there was a natural sense,
as though she sensed
what the stars say
what the birds say
what the wind and the clouds say
a sense of soul and self,
that African sense.
"And work like you're building
something of your own," she'd say.
Full time. Over time. All the time.
No nonsense.
and she raised me like she raised four of her own

who were like her
in a good many good ways.
Which showed up in my mother
who was truly her mother's daughter
and still her own person
And i was hurt and scared and shocked
when Lily Scott left suddenly one night,
and they sent a limousine from heaven
to take her to God if there is one.
So i knew she had gone.
And i came from a broken home.

So on the streets of New York
the family, me and my mother,
moved on through my teens
where all the ologists'
hypothetical theoretical
analytical hypocritical
will not be able to factor
why i failed to commit
the obligatory robbery, burglary,
murder or rape.
Nor know that i was
fighting my way out of the ghetto.
But i lived in the projects without becoming one,
shot jumpers in the park
instead of people,
went to a school that
informed instead of reformed
read books without getting booked
and had a couple of jobs
to help with the surgery on my broken home.

And so my life has been guided
and all the love i needed was provided
and through my mother's sacrifices I saw where her life went
to give more than birth to me, but life to me.
And this ain't one of them cliches

about Black women being strong
'cause hell! If you're weak, you're gone!
But life courage, determined to do more than just survive.
Say what? Of course she had a choice:
Don't do it! Work.
Raining cold mornings, dirty streets
and dirty Goddamn people
worrying her way up rickety ass stairs
working for Welfare...
I'm sorry if I'm drifting on
but this is all I know about a broken home:
And she sings better than I do
and I listen to her and B.B. manhandle Handel. [Joke]

And hey amigo!
17th and 8th in the park.
13th and 9th in the dark:
congas, cowbells, bongoes and salsa,
beer cans, Ripple and good herbs.
Willie Bobo, Eddie Palmieri, Ray Barreto
and the Mayor of my neighborhood
long before he covered "The Bottle," Joe Bataan.
Mi madre estudia in
La Universidad de San Juan
y vivia en San Turce
y mi madre vivia en Barranquitas

Yeah. Raised by women,
but they were not alone
because the chain of truth was not broken
in Bob Scott's home.
And my mother's name is Bob, Robert,
Bobbie Scott-Heron
and saying thank you, I love you ain't enough.

My life has been balanced on that razor's edge of Gods rolling dice
and it seemed as though they had a job for me to do:

Because the Rambler got totaled in Avondale and
Geoffrey's Ford four o'clock soloing
through a D.C. slalom when the brakes locked
steel and wheels a la lamppost.
Good morning!
And the white preacher, Reverend Cockcroft,
who grabbed me when I treaded on the bottom of Lake Kiamesha.

And i am small remembering how
she showed me more caring and sharing than i deserved;
more courage and daring than i have.
The ONLY ONE who has ALWAYS been on my side.
And too many homes have a missing woman or man
without the feeling of missing love.
Maybe there are homes that are hurt,
but there are no REAL LIVES that hurt will not reach.
But not broken.
Unless the homes of soldiers stationed overseas
or lost in battles are broken.
Unless the homes of firemen, policemen, construction workers,
seamen, railroad men, truckers, pilots who lost their lives,
but not what their lives stood for.
Because men die, lose, are lost and leave.
And so do women.
I come from WHAT THEY CALLED A BROKEN HOME,
but if they had ever really called at our house
they would have known how wrong they were.
We were working on our lives
and our homes and dealing with what we had,
not what we didn't have.
My life has been guided by women
but because of them i am a Man.
God bless you, Mama. And thank you.

The "Movie" Poems

In February 1981, I went on a Black History Month tour that took me to some of the nation's most prominent campuses and communities.

There were two things in particular that people everywhere wanted to talk about: First, I had just completed a most enjoyable and successful four month tour with the #1 entertainer-composer-musician Stevie Wonder, which had included, on January 15th, a rally in Washington, D.C. in support of Dr. King's birthday becoming a national holiday.

"What were the chances? How many people were REALLY there? What sort of a brother was Stevie to just be around?"

Second, what were my feelings about the election of President Reagan?

Discussions concerning the second question started to become my first topic during the February lectures. A description of the conditions that paved the way for Mr. Reagan's election AND what I viewed as the conditions created by his victory.

In April, while working with a man I also consider a creative genius, musician-engineer Malcolm Cecil, the idea of the poem (Part Two) without setting the stage, so to speak (with an introduction), didn't feel right for a recording. And there was also a line from a tune I kept hearing that I felt needed to be included:

"This ain't really your life, ain't really your life, ain't really, ain't really nothing but a movie." The tune became Part 3 on the album *Reflections*.

And armed with a bunch of words, a vague structure and my ace-in-the-studio, Malcolm, "B Movie" was born.

And, in 1984 when it became clear that the President would be running again, it was time for another round. However, I felt as though my friends, and even my enemies, would be let down if we decided to do "B Movie II," or even "B Movie Also (Too)." I was glad to find that art can imitate art, even when "it ain't really your life" — which is why II, 2 or TOO became "Re-Ron."

Part One

"B" Movie
Introduction

The first thing I want to say is "Mandate, my ass!"

Because it seems as though we've been convinced that 26% of the registered voters, not even 26% of the American people, but 26% of the registered voters form a mandate, or a landslide. 21% voted for "Skippy" and 3 or 4% voted for someone else who might have been running.

And yes I do remember (in this year that we have declared to be from "Shogun to Raygun"), I remember what I said about Raygun: "I called him 'Hollyweird'. Acted like an actor. Acted like a liberal. Acted like General Franco when he acted like Governor of California. That's after he started acting like a Republican. Then (in 1976) acted like somebody was going to vote for him for President."

Now he acted like 26% of the registered voters is actually a mandate. We're all actors in this I suppose.

What has happened is that in the last 20 years America has changed from a producer to a consumer. And all consumers know that when the producer names the tune the consumer has got to dance. That's the way it is. We used to be producers and were very inflexible at that. Now that we are consumers we find things difficult to understand.

Natural resources and minerals will change your world. The Arabs used to be in the Third World. They have bought the Second World and put a firm down payment on the First one. Controlling your resources will control your world.

This country has been surprised by the way the world looks now. They don't know if they want to be diplomats or continue the policy of nuclear nightmare diplomacy. John Foster Dulles ain't nothing but the name of an airport now.

America wants Nostalgia. They want to go back as far as they can, even if it turns out to be only last week. Not to face now or the future, but to face backwards. And yesterday was the time of our cinema heroes riding to the rescue at the last minute; the day of the man on the white horse or the man in the white hat, coming to save America at the last moment. Someone always came to save America at the last moment.

And when America found itself having a hard time facing the future they looked for one of their heroes. Someone like John Wayne. But unfortunately John Wayne was no longer available, so they settled for Ronald the Raygun.

And it has turned into something that we can only look at like a "B" movie.

Part Two

"B" Movie —The Poem

Come with us back to those inglorious days before heroes were zeros. Before fair was square. When the cavalry came straight-away and all American men were like Hemingway, to the days of the wondrous "B" movie.

The Producer, underwritten by all the millionaires necessary, will be "Casper" the defensive Weinburger. No more animated a choice is avail -able.

The director will be "Attila" the Haig, running around declaring himself "In charge and in control!" The ultimate realization of inmates taking over at the asylum.

The screenplay will be adapted from the book called *Voodoo Economics* by George "Papa Doc" Bush.

The theme song will be done by The Village People. That most military tune "Macho Man." A theme song for saber rattling and selling wars door-to-door. Remember, we're looking for the closest thing we can find to John Wayne.

Cliches abound like kangaroos courtesy of some spaced out Marlin Perkins, a Raygun contemporary. Cliches like:

"Tall in the saddle." Like "Riding on or off into the sunset." Like "Qadafi, get off my planet by sunset." More so than "He died with his boots on."

Marine tough, the man is Bogart tough, Cagney tough and Hollywood tough, the man is John Wayne tough, the man is cheap steak tough and Bonzo substantial.

A Madison Avenue masterpiece. A miracle, a cotton candy politician: "Presto Macho!"

Put your orders in, America, and quick as Kodak we duplicate, with the accent on the dupe!

It's a clear case of selective amnesia: remembering what we want to remember and forgetting what we choose to forget. All of a sudden the man who called for a bloodbath on our college campuses is supposed to be Dudley Goddamn Do-Right?

"You go give them liberals hell, Ronny! That was the mandate to the new Captain Bligh on the new Ship of Fools.

Obviously based on chameleon performances of the past: as a liberal Democrat. As the head of the Screen Actor's Guild. When other celluloid saviours were cringing in terror from McCarthyism Ron stood tall!

It goes all the way back from Hollywood to Hillbillies, from liberal to libelous, from Bonzo to Birchite to Born Again.

Civil Rights. Gay Rights. Women's rights. They're all wrong! Call in the cavalry to disrupt this perception of freedom gone wild. First one of them wants freedom and then the whole damn world wants freedom!

Nostalgia. That's what America wants. The good old days. When we "gave them hell!" When the buck stopped somewhere and you could still buy something with it! To a time when movies were in black and white and so was everything else.

Let us go back to the campaign trail before six gun Ron shot off his face and developed Hoof in Mouth. Before the free press went down before a full court press and were reluctant to view the menu because they knew that the only meal available was "crow".

Lon Chaney, our man of 1,000 faces got nothing on Ron.

Doug Henning will do the makeup.

Special effects by Grecian Formula 16 and Crazy Glue.

Transportation furnished by the David Rockefeller Remote Control Company. Their slogan is: "Why wait til 1984. You can panic now and avoid the rush."

So much for the good news. As Wall Street goes so goes the nation and here's a look at the closing stocks:

Racism is up. Human Rights are down. Peace is shaky. War items are hot. The House claims all ties. Jobs are down, money is scarce and Common Sense is at an all time low with heavy trading.

Movies were looking better than ever and now no one is looking because we're all starring in a "B" movie. And we would have rather had John Wayne. In fact, we would have done better with John Wayne.

Part Three

Re-Ron

Ah yes, they're off and running again. The campaign trail. And doesn't he look like himself? Back in the saddle again.

From Roy Rogers to Buck Rogers to Ginger Rogers to Kenny Rogers to Mr. Rogers to Jolly Rogers. A Re-Ron.

From Gabby Hayes to Rutherford B. Hayes to Helen Hayes to Isaac Hayes to walking around in a bleeping Haze. A Re-Ron.

In the dead of night we've seen it all: Boy George in drag? Or was Maggie Thatcher RayGun in drag?

Maggie and Jiggs. What gigs they got. That's the problem.

It's a Re-Ron. It's Geritol. It's Jerry Mahoney and off the bleeping wall.

He's terrorized and jeopardized and severed ties and sent our spies to plant them mines and told them lies all for the bottom line.

We don't need no Re-Ron.

We don't need no Re-Ron, you know.

We don't need no Re-Ron.

We've seen all the Re-Rons before.

But there he is. Running again. Re-running. Re-ronning. It's a Re-Ron.

A Re-Ron as predicted before the RayGun threats were world wide inflicted.

All those recent damages and nerve changes. Re-freezing the cold war and lighting a fire under the hot one.

Banging on the war drums and we're listening to the rhythms.

It's a Re-Ron. Milton Berle.

The Duke of Wayne. The Duke of Earl.

Orson Welles doing "War of the Worlds".

The Hardy Boys and Georgy Girl.

It's a Re-Ron. A corruption piece starring

Raymond Donovan and Edwin Meese.

It's a Re-Ron. The Latin Plan

and here's our star: Nacho Man!

11

We don't need no Re-Ron.
We don't need no Re-Ron, you know.
We don't need no Re-Ron.
We've seen all the Re-Rons before.

It's beyond real-to-reel and Shogun to RayGun.
And no one has been psyched by cosmetic set changes and minimal shuffling of the deck of the cast of characters:
[I was glad to see James Watt go.]
Secretary of the Inferior. James "kilowatt," Kill a Tree, Kill a Seal!
Attila The Haig transformed into Peanuts. Called Shultz on Capitol Hill.
A dead ringer for the Cowardly Lion from *The Wizard of Oz*. And every time I see him I hear the song:
"We're off to see the Arabs. Off to see the Arabs."
Or just off. And up the yellow brick road. Another war drummer from the Cap Weinburger school of arms pushing overkill and The Henry
Kissinger Peace Academy
We don't need no Re-Ron.
We don't need no Re-Ron, you know.
We don't need no Re-Ron.
We've seen all the Re-Rons before.

And through it all we closed our eyes at 33 and 1/3, didn't we?
Going down for the 3rd time under the 3rd degree.
A 3rd of our fellow Americans breaking their backs for 3rd class
citizenship,
taking a 3rd less home on payday because of inflation
while 30 years after segregation
was tried, found guilty and banished from the nation
when here it comes again: Discrimination!
And the world watching our response to the 3rd World because the stakes
are the 3rd World War!:
It's the neutron bomb for Lebanon.
He's the gladiator invader of Grenada!
There's millions more for El Salvador!
and he's up to his "Keisters" with the Sandanistas!
Would we take Fritz (Mondale) without Grits (Carter)?
We'd take Fritz the Cat.

12

Would we take Jesse Jackson?
Hell, we'd take Michael Jackson!
We don't need no Re-Ron.
We don't need no Re-Ron, you know.
We don't need no Re-Ron.
We've seen all the Re-Rons before.

A Re-ron, the late late show.
A black and white flick from ages ago.
A Re-Ron. The late late show.
Ain't we seen this flick somewhere before?

And then there's stage presence. My, doesn't he look like himself?
A Re-Ron:
The face never changes nor political stance.
He's constantly smiling, a Greek comedy mask.
So cool on the camera. The hair's in place.
The same old lines and the same cliches.
Perfectly rehearsed. Obscuring wrong and right.
He says he's defending some bull____ while he's picking a fight.
It's a Re-Ron, a time machine
stuck in reverse and filming new scenes.
20 years gone at the point of a gun.
To hell with reality: "Places everyone!"
It's a Re-Ron. Nostalgia got stoned.
Mom and apple pie.
No place like home.
And leave it to Beaver and the Twilight Zone.
Can't they face it, Goddamnit? Yesterday's gone.

We don't need no Re-Ron.
We don't need no Re-Ron, you know
We don't need no Re-Ron.
We've seen all the Re-Rons before.

A Re-Ron. The late late show. A black and white flick from ages ago.
A Re-Ron. The late late show
starring Curly, the RayGun, Larry and Moe.
Like a Saturday morning cartoon show. Like a migraine headache you had
before. Cinematic garbaggio.
We don't need no Re-Ron!
We don't need no Re-Ron.

Space Shuttle

Space was the place
where at least we thought our dreams were safe;
where yesterdays of youth and innocence and grace
floated somewhere high above the planet's face.
Ah, but the distance has been erased
'cause Uncle Sam is on the case.
E.T. is joining the Arm's Race!
They're up there building some kinda military base.
Rocketing through the atmosphere,
sliding into second gear
while miles below the people cheer
the New Invaders on the New Frontier.
...but there are also those who do not cheer
The gravity of their lives appears
and in their eyes flash frozen fears
while rocket sounds are all they hear.

Space Shuttle/ raising hell down on the ground!
Space Shuttle/ turning the seasons upside down.
Space Shuttle/ and all the hungry people know
all change sho' 'nuff ain't progress when you're poor.
No matter what man goes looking for
he always seems to find a war.
As soon as dreams of peace are felt
the war is raging somewhere else.

We must have somehow been disarmed
or lost our heads over false alarms;
underwhelmed and over charmed,
watching the storm clouds from afar.
Exploration, proliferation,
spending more while pockets fill.
Assessments of our investments
drive us on to Overkill.
Practice looks of great surprise

as the Captain Kirk of "Free Enterprise."
Wall Street says "Let's play Defense!"
and "Dollar bills make damn good sense!"
Hail to the new Protectionism!
Let's bring on the new age of Humanism.
We can put the cap on Capitalism!
We've got a giant, mechanical Ray-gunism!

Space Shuttle/ raising hell down on the ground!
Space Shuttle/ turning the seasons upside down.
Space Shuttle/ and all the hungry people know
all change sho' 'nuff ain't progress when you're poor.
No matter what man goes looking for
he always seems to find a war.
As soon as dreams of peace are felt
the war is raging somewhere else.

Space was the rage
so Hollyweird took center stage
and together we wondered whether
we would ever get over the weather.
Things started happening that seemed so strange,
like the whole jet stream is being rearranged:
There was a clear day in L.A.,
a foot of snow in Tampa Bay.
The space shuttle no sooner goes up
than we watch while the Weather Man goes nuts

Tornados and hurricanes,
dead rivers and Acid Rain,
volcanoes ages dead
suddenly just get up and lose their heads.
Typhoons, monsoons,
and tidal waves come down from an angry moon.
It's earthquaking all the Goddamn time
and the only common denominator we can find...

Space Shuttle/ raising hell down on the ground!
Space Shuttle/ turning the seasons upside down.
Space Shuttle/ and all the hungry people know
all change sho' 'nuff ain't progress when you're poor.
No matter what man goes looking for
he always seems to find a war.
As soon as dreams of peace are felt
the war is raging somewhere else.

Old folks must have had it right
from the time they saw the first satellite
they said "Some advancements may be good,
but not in God's neighborhood."
Laser beams and moonbeams,
we got peace dreams killed by war schemes,
there's a hole shot through the Ozone layer
that has put the fear back into atmos-fear.
ICBM, MX, Cruise Missiles,
obsolete today.
Let's spend another billion on The Sergeant York
and then throw that "sumbitch" away.
War is big business without a doubt
so there ain't much chance of peace breaking out.
Underwater, overhead, God we'll all be nervous wrecks
'cause did you hear where they're going next?

Space Shuttle/ raising hell down on the ground!
Space Shuttle/ turning the seasons upside down.
Space shuttle/ and all the hungry people know
all change sho' 'nuff ain't progress when you're poor.
No matter what man goes looking for
he always seems to find a war.
As soon as dreams of peace are felt
the war is raging somewhere else.

Black History

I was wondering about our yesterdays
and started digging through the rubble
and to tell the truth somebody went
to a hell of a lot of trouble
to make sure that when we looked things up
we wouldn't fare too well
and that we would come up with totally unreliable
pictures of ourselves.
But I've compiled what few facts I could,
I mean, such as they are
to see if I could shed a little bit of light
and this is what I got so far:
First, white folks discovered Africa
and claimed it fair and square.
Cecil Rhodes couldn't have been robbing nobody
'cause he said there was nobody there.
White folks brought all of the civilization
since there wasn't none around.
They said "How could these folks be civilized
when you never see nobody writing nothing down?"
And to prove all of their suspicions
it didn't take too long.
They found out there were whole groups of people
--in plain sight!--
running around with no clothes on. That's right!
The women, the men, the young and the old,
righteous white folks covered their eyes.
So no time was spent considering the environment.
Hell no! This here, this just wasn't civilized.
And another way they knew we were backwards,
or at least this is how we were taught,
is that "Unlike the very civilized people of Europe"
these Black groups actually fought!

And yes! They were some "rather crude implements"
and yes! there was "primitive art"
and yes! they were masters of hunting and fishing
and courtesy came from the heart.
And yes! there was medicine, love and religion,
inter-tribal communication by drum.
But no papers and pencils and other utensils
and hell, these folks never even heard of a gun.
So this is why the colonies came
to stabilize the land.
Because The Dark Continent had copper and gold
and the discoverers had themselves a plan.
They would "discover" all the places with promise.
You didn't need no titles or deeds.
You could just appoint people to make everything legal,
to sanction the trickery and greed.
And out in the bushes if the natives got restless
You could call that "guerilla attack!"
And never have to describe that somebody finally got
wise
and decided they wanted their things back.
But still we are victims of word games,
semantics is always a bitch:
Places once called underdeveloped and "backwards"
are now called "mineral rich."
And still it seems the game goes on
with unity always just out of reach
because Libya and Egypt used to be in Africa,
but they've been moved to the "Middle East."
There are examples galore I assure you,
but if interpreting was left up to me
I'd be sure every time folks knew this version wasn't
mine
which is why it is called "His story."

The World

The world!
Planet Earth; third from the Sun of a gun, 360 degrees.
And as new worlds emerge
stay alert. Stay aware.
Watch the Eagle! Watch the Bear!
Earthquaking, foundation shaking,
bias breaking, new day making
change.
Accumulating, liberating, educating, stimulating change!
Tomorrow was born yesterday.
From inside the rib or people cage
the era of our first blood stage was blotted or erased
or TV screened or defaced.
Remember there's a revolution going on in the world.
One blood of the early morning
revolves to the one idea of our tomorrow.
Home boy, hold on!
Now more than ever all the family must come together.
Ideas of freedom and harmony, great civilizations
yesterday brought today will bring tomorrow.
We must be about
earth quaking, liberating, investigating
and new day making change in
The world

What You See Ain't What You Goetz

I get the sho' 'nuff blues
checkin' out The Daily News
no matter which way it's comin' from
I'm told I'm not supposed to choose
just accept the newsman's views
but that sho' ain't no happy medium

You see all I want is the facts
but blow dried hairdos is gettin' into the act
because reporters are expert observers
they establish social trends
decidin' who's out and who's in
and rush in with the tragedies that unnerve us:

Syndicated columnists
lookin' to get their asses kissed
cause they're the big shots of political affairs
and the anchorman's job
is to look extra suave
while they're trying to convince us that they care
while the radio commentator
is a five minute narrator
whose news is perpetually grim
and his ego is blown
he's got a great baritone
but the cameras ain't never on him

But the message is clear
they want all Black folks to hear
that the price you got to pay to be free
you get told how to feel
you get told what is real
to be exactly how they want you to be:
you get the rational logical

sound philosophical
poetic distortions
political contortions
cause white folks still ain't ready yet
so what you hear ain't gonna be what you get

Now some folks may call me a radical
or remind me that at best I'm not practical
to keep pointing out what everyone should know.
But we're still looking for justice
while other folks devise ways to bust us
so we spend more time in court than McEnroe.

Because when the time for freedom came
folks started feeling only the surface had changed
instead of celebrating "Free at last!"
'Cause all the racists had said "Okay"
because equality can work both ways
and they promptly started kicking poor white folks ass.

And said:
How can the issue be race
when every citizen can take his or her case
and be heard by a jury of their peers?
meanwhile I'm listening to the rundown
about four young brothers who was gunned down
by some psycho with imaginary fears.

Check it out:
When you get down to the real nitty-gritty
you're on a subway in New York City
and Bernhard, the gunman, shows upon the set.
And he decides these four young Blacks
are about to launch an attack
though they hadn't attacked nobody yet.

Regardless, Bernie makes his play
and he's like Eastwood saying "Make my fuckin' day!" and
in self defense he even shoots someone wounded on the floor.
Then he confesses on video tape,
but since he was in an "agitated state"
He's acquitted and let out to shoot some more.

Now does this mean every sister and brother
Mexican, Indian, Oriental or other
won't ever see homicide put them behind bars?
Because it legitimately terrifies me
to know that the next sumbitch I see
might be armed and just as crazy as Bernhard.

Or is this proof that the system works
or are we all being treated like jerks
Take your chance and step right up to place your bets.
And I'm gonna put my money down
saying if it's ever the other way around
we'll find out that what you see ain't what you Goetz.

Thought Out

we just thought it was a drink,
but maybe had there been more time to think...
a cognac on the rocks and a glass of white wine
crowd thinning out cause it's near closing time
laughs, cigarette smoke, an adult's playroom
where foreplay for players who like adult freedom
and dimly dark lowlight sparks...
we just thought it was different
like a pleasant surprise
and maybe we wouldn't have said so much as "hello"
had we looked around into other folks' eyes
we just thought it was cool
but not the rigid, frigid,
frozen, not-chosen
  petrified, paralyzed
  ossified ostracized
put out to pasture is the ultimate disaster
we just thought it was a glance
almost something thought to yourself
a second look, a double give and take
a "very nice, my lady" and/or
an appraisal of the up-closer, "Hmm"
we thought it was a change of pace
an hour away, a quiet someplace
just to talk, walk, speak, peek
see behind that sudden jolt,
an electric unexpected volts
probably nothing but might be fun
if not, nobody lost nobody won
but much more suddenly than all at once,
an unexpected cloud that blocks the sun
and before we heard the starter's gun
too soon to know it was too late to run
we thought it was no big deal
we thought it had an ugly feel

a curious, furious over reaction
that there would be no end to the distractions
unless we gave up
and said we'd had enough
and we had thought it was ours.

The Oldest Reason in the World

...because I always feel like running.
not away,
...because there's no such place.
...because if there was
i would have found it by now
...because it's easier to run; easier than staying
and finding out you're the only one who didn't run
...because running will be the way your life and mine
will be described:
as in the long run or
as in having given someone a run for his money or
as in running out of time
...because running makes me look like everyone else
though i hope there will never
be cause for that
...because i will be running in the other direction:
not running for cover;
...because if i knew where cover was
i would stay there and never have to run for it.
not running for my life
...because i have to be running
for something of more value to be running
and not in fear;
...because the thing i fear cannot be
escaped, eluded, avoided,
hidden from, protected from, gotten away from,
not without showing the fear
as i see it now
...because closer, clearer/no sir nearer
...because of you, and
...because of the nice that you
quietly, quickly be causing and

...because you're going to see me run soon, and
...because you're going to know why i'm running.
then.
you'll know then
...because i'm not going to tell you now.

Lady Day and John Coltrane

Ever feel kinda down and out and don't know
   just what to do?
Livin' alla your days in darkness, let the sun shine
   through.
Ever feel that somehow, somewhere you lost
   your way?
And if you don't get help you won't make it
   through the day.
You could call on Lady Day!
You could call on John Coltrane!
They'll wash your troubles, your troubles away.

Plastic people with plastic minds on their way to
   plastic homes.
There's no beginning, there ain't no ending
just on and on and on and on and...
It's all because we're so afraid to say that we're
   alone
until our hero rides in, rides in on his
   saxophone.
You could call on Lady Day!
You could call on John Coltrane!
They'll wash your troubles, your troubles away.

I Think I'll Call It Morning

I'm gonna take myself a piece of sunshine
and paint it all over my sky.
Be no rain. Be no rain.
I'm gonna take the song from every bird
and make them sing it just for me.
Be no rain.
And I think I'll call it morning from now on.
Why should I survive on sadness/
convince myself I've got to be alone?
Why should I subscribe to this world's
  madness
knowing that I've got to live on?

I think I'll call it morning from now on.
I'm gonna take myself a piece of sunshine
and paint it all over my sky.
Be no rain. Be no rain.
I'm gonna take the song from every bird
and make them sing it just for me.
Why should I hang my head?
Why should I let tears fall from my eyes
when I've seen everything that there is to see
and I know that there ain't no sense in crying!
    I know that there ain't no sense in crying!
I think I'll call it morning from now on.

No Knock
(to be slipped into John Mitchell's Suggestion Box)

You explained it to me John I must admit,
but just for the record you was talkin' shit!
Long raps about No Knock being legislated
for the people you've always hated
in this hell-hole that you/we all call "home."
"No knock!" The Man will say, "to keep that man
    from beatin' his wife!"
"No Knock! The Man will say, "to keep people
    from hurtin' themselves!"
No-knockin', head rockin', enter shockin',
    shootin', cussin',
killin', cryin', lyin' and bein' white!
No knocked on my brother, Fred Hampton,
bullet holes all over the place!
No knocked on my brother, Michael Harris,
and jammed a shotgun against his skull!
For my protection?
Who's gonna protect me from you?
The likes of you! The nerve of you!
To talk that shit face-to-face
your tomato face dead pan
your dead pan deadening another freedom plan!
No knockin', head rockin', enter shockin',
    shootin', cussin',
killin', cryin', lyin' and bein' white!
But if you're wise, No Knocker,
you'll tell your no-knockin' lackies
to No Knock on my brother's heads
and No Knock on my sister's heads
and double lock your door
because soon someone may be No Knocking...
    for you!

Billy Green is Dead

"The economy's in an uproar,
the whole damn country's in the red,
taxi fares is goin' up...What?
You say Billy Green is dead?"
"The government can't decide on busin'
Or at least that's what they said.
Yeah, I heard when you tol' me,
You said Billy Green is dead."
"But let me tell you 'bout these hotpants
that this big-legged sista wore
when I partied with the frat boys.
You say Billy took an overdose?"
"Well now, junkies will be junkies,
But did you see Gunsmoke las' night?
Man they had themselves a shootout
an' folks wuz dyin' left and right!
At the end when Matt was cornered
I had damn near give up hope...
Why you keep on interruptin' me?
You say my son is takin' dope?
Call a lawyer! Call a doctor!
What you mean I shouldn't scream?
My only son is on narcotics,
should I stand here like I'm pleased?"
Is that familiar anybody?
Check out what's inside your head,
because it never seems to matter
when it's Billy Green who's dead.

Winter is a metaphor — a term used not only to describe the season of ice, but this period of our lives through which we are traveling.

In our hearts we feel that Spring is just around the corner; a Spring of brotherhood and united spirits among people of color. Everyone is moving, searching. There is a restlessness within our souls that keeps us questioning, discovering, struggling against a system that will not allow us space and time for fresh expression. Western Icemen have attempted to distort time.

We approach Winter, the most depressing period in the history of his Western Empire, with threats of oil shortages and energy crises. But we, as Black people, have been a source of endless energy, endless beauty and endless determination. I have many things to tell you about tomorrow's love and light. We will see you in the Spring.

In the interest of national security, please help us carry out our constitutional duty to overthrow the king.

Notes from *Winter In America* (10/73)

32

Winter in America

From the Indians who welcomed the pilgrims
to the buffalo who once ruled the plains;
like the vultures circling beneath the dark clouds
looking for the rain/looking for the rain.
From the cities that stagger on the coast lines
in a nation that just can't take much more/
like the forest buried beneath the highways
never had a chance to grow/never had a chance
    to grow.
It's winter; winter in america
and all of the healers have been killed or forced
    away.
It's winter; winter in america
and ain't nobody fighting 'cause nobody knows
    what to save.
The con-stitution was a noble piece of paper;
with Free Society they struggled but they died in
    vain/
and now Democracy is ragtime on the corner
hoping that it rains/hoping that it rains.
And I've seen the robins perched in barren
    treetops
watching last ditch racists marching across the
    floor
and like the peace signs that melted in our
    dreams
never had a chance to grow/never had a
    chance to grow.
it's winter; winter in america
and all of the healers done been killed or put in
    jail
it's winter, winter in america
and ain't nobody fighting 'cause nobody knows
    what to save.

The Bottle

See that Black boy over there, runnin' scared
his ol' man's in a bottle.
He done quite his 9 to 5 to drink full time
so now he's livin' in the bottle.
See that Black boy over there, runnin' scared
his 'ol man got a problem.
Pawned off damn near everything, his ol'
  woman's weddin' ring for a bottle.
And don't you think it's a crime
when time after time, people in the bottle.

See that sista, sho wuz fine before she
started drinkin' wine
from the bottle.
Said her ol' man committed a crime
and he's doin' time,
so now she's in the bottle.
She's out there on the avenue, all by herself
sho' needs help from the bottle.
Preacherman tried to help her out,
she cussed him out and hit him in the head with a bottle.
And don't you think it's a crime
when time after time, people in the bottle.

See that gent in the wrinkled suit
he done damn near blown his cool
to the bottle
He wuz a doctor helpin' young girls along
if they wuzn't too far gone to have problems.
But defenders of the dollar eagle
Said "What you doin', Doc, it ain't legal,"
and now he's in the bottle.
Now we watch him everyday tryin' to
chase the pigeons away
from the bottle.
And don't you think it's a crime
when time after time, people in the bottle.

Johannesburg

What's the word?
Tell me brother, have you heard
   from Johannesburg?
What's the word?
Sister/woman have you heard
   from Johannesburg?
They tell me that our brothers over there
are defyin' the Man.
We don't know for sure because the news we
   get
is unreliable, man.
Well I hate it when the blood starts flowin',
but I'm glad to see resistance growin'.
Somebody tell me what's the word?
Tell me brother, have you heard
   from Johannesburg?
They tell me that our brothers over there
   refuse to work in the mines.
They may not get the news but they need to know
we're on their side.
Now sometimes distance brings
   misunderstanding,
but deep in my heart I'm demanding:
Somebody tell me what's the word?
Sister/woman have you heard
   'bout Johannesburg?
I know that their strugglin' over there
ain't gonna free me,
but we all need to be strugglin'
if we're gonna be free.
Don't you wanna be free?

Pieces of a Man

be no bargain-day xtras on freedom and
ain't nobody givin' it away.
echoes from overloud voices get trapped
  inside
badass black thunderclouds and carried to God
who sits at the corner of forever.
God sent down correctly.
God sent down right on timely:
music-muzac-muzick
soulfulsoothings soulfulmournings
messages that cannot be decoded by stale
  brains
bluesgospeljazzrhythmscreamingshouting—
  blasting serene
words and notes that mean:
inside you is where life is and not at a wool-
  worthless 5 & 10.
the message is here; inside the man
bubbling brain cells and heart/soul cells
ax-cell-er-rating faster until understood
and used and passed on and used and passed
  on and used and...

...mid-winter
There is a revolution going on in America/the
World; a shifting in the winds/vibrations, as disruptive
as an actual earth-tremor, but it is happening in
our hearts.

There is a revolution going on in America/the
World; a change as swift as blackening skies when
the rains come, as fresh and clear as the air after the
rain. We need change.

The seeds of this revolution were planted hun-
dreds of years ago; in slave ships, in cotton fields, in
tepees, in the souls of brave men. The seeds were
watered, nurtured and bloom now in our hands as
we rock our babies.

It is mid-winter in America; a man-made season of
shattered dreams and shocked citizens, fumbling
and frustrated beneath the crush of greed of
corporate monsters and economic manipulators
gone wild. There are bitter winds born in the
knowledge of secret plans hatched by Western
Money Men that backfired and grew out of control
to eat its own.

We must support ourselves and stand fast
together even as pressure disperses our enemies
and bangs at our doors. No one can do everything,
but everybody can do something. We must all do
what we can for each other to weather this blizzard.
Now more than ever all the family must be
together; to comfort, to protect, to guide, to survive
because...there is a revolution going on in
America/ the World.

Notes from *First Minute of a New Day* (1/75)

Small Talk at 125th and Lenox

Tell me:

Did'ja ever eat corn bread an' black-eyed peas?
Or watermelon and mustard greens?
Get high as you can on Saturday night
and then go to church on Sunday to set things
right?

Listen:

"I seen Miz Blake after Willie yesterday.
She'd a killed anybody who'd a got in her way!
Hey look! I got a tv for a pound on the head.
Jimmy Gene got the bes' Panamanian Red.
No, I ain't got on no underclothes,
But the Hawk got to get through this Gypsy Rose!
I think Clay got his very good points.
You say a trey bag wit' thirteen joints?
Who cares if LBJ is in town?
Up with Stokely an' H. Rap Brown!
I dunno if the riots is wrong,
But Whitey been kickin' my ass fo' too long.
I wuz s'pose to baby but they hel' my pay
Did you hear what the number wuz yesterday?
Junkies is all right when they ain't broke.
They leaves you alone when they high on dope.
Damn, but I wish I could get up an' move!
Shut up, hell, you know that ain't true."

Paint It Black

Picture a man of nearly thirty
who seems twice as old with clothes torn and
   dirty.
Give him a job shining shoes
or cleaning out toilets with bus station crews.
Give him six children with nothing to eat.
Expose them to life on a ghetto street.
Tie an old rag around his wife's head and
have her pregnant and lying in bed.
Stuff them all in a Harlem house.
Then tell them how bad things are down South.

Bridging

I thought i saw last night
across a ridge,
an ebony bridge that spanned all chasms from
      Harlem to Home.
African!
      Zimbabwe with apartheid still.
Kenya, prove the Black man's will.
Biafra, the division is not yet killed.
African!
      Queen's English, manners so defined
      Wardrobe styled and dignified
      Darker skin and no Tarzan smile.
Afro-American!
      Handshake and dashikis too
      James Brown doin' the soul boogaloo
      People starving with nothing to do.
Afro-American!
      Idolizing TV-man
      Capitalism's also-ran
      Colloquialism's cool man.
African! from the continent
Afro-Americans! from the discontent
Brothers! can we not implement
      a bit of faith?
      a bit of love?
For we are all truly brothers
From the womb of mother same
From the genesis we were one
Let us be one, once again.

The Vulture

Standing in the ruins of another Black man's life,
Or flying through the valley separating day and
 night.
"I am death," cried the Vulture. "For the people
 of the light."
Charon brought his raft from the sea that sails
 on souls,
And saw the scavenger departing, taking warm
 hearts to the cold.
He knew the ghetto was the haven for the
 meanest creature ever known.
In a wilderness of heartbreak and a desert of
 despair,
Evil's clarion of justice shrieks a cry of naked
 terror.
Taking babies from their mamas and leaving
 grief beyond compare.
So if you see the Vulture coming, flying circles in
 your mind,
Remember there is no escaping for he will
 follow close behind.
Only promise me a battle, battle for your soul
 and mine.

Whitey on the Moon

A rat done bit my sister Nell.
  (with Whitey on the moon)
Her face and arms began to swell.
  (and Whitey's on the moon)
I can't pay no doctor bill.
  (but Whitey's on the moon)
Ten years from now I'll be payin' still.
  (while Whitey's on the moon)
The man jus' upped my rent las' night.
  ('cause Whitey's on the moon)
No hot water, no toilets, no lights.
  (but Whitey's on the moon)
I wonder why he uppin' me?
  ('cause Whitey's on the moon?)
I wuz already payin' 'im fifty a week.
  (with Whitey on the moon)
Taxes takin' my whole damn check,
Junkies make me a nervous wreck,
The price of food is goin' up,
An' as if all that crap wuzn't enough:
A rat done bit my sister Nell.
  (with Whitey on the moon)
Her face an' arm began to swell.
  (but Whitey's on the moon)
Was all that money I made las' year
  (for Whitey on the moon?)
How come there ain't no money here?
  (Hmm! Whitey's on the moon)
Y'know I jus' 'bout had my fill
  (of Whitey on the moon.)
I think I'll sen' these doctor bills
  (To Whitey on the moon.)

*Free will is free mind. Free to evaluate the
systems that control our lives from without and
free to examine the emotions that control our
perspective from within.*

*Black people everywhere are becoming aware
of the gaps that exist between the "American"
values and the values of our spirits. The nature of
our spirits demand a life-style apart from the
American life speed — a lifestyle that accents life
and not death, love and not hate.*

*We have things to do for tomorrow. Our
children will have to deal with all the mistakes we
make today. To live in dignity they will have to
erase many of the personal compromises we
made. We must actively search out the truth and
help each other.*

*We do not need more legislation or more
liberals. What we need is self love and self respect.
By every means necessary!*

*Unfortunately, it is not easy to love yourself after
you heard
hatred and self destruction in every city. We must
make the extra effort needed to identify the true
enemies of our peace of mind.*

*We can begin by realizing that though we are
trapped by economic and geographical boundaries,
we are still capable of spiritual freedom
supported by the truth.*

*What we do with the truth is the key to our
freedom.*

Notes from *Reflection on Free Will* (5/15/72)
"...words are important for the mind/notes are
for the soul."
(from "Plastic Pattern People," 11/67)

43

Plastic Pattern People

glad to get high and see the slow motion world,
just to reach and touch the half-notes floating.
world spinning quicker than 9/8 Dave Brubeck. we
       come now frantically searching for Thomas
       More rainbow villages.
       up on suddenly Charlie Mingus and Ahmed
          Abdul-Malik
to add bass to a bottomless pit of insecurity. you
       may be plastic because
you never meditate about the bottom of glasses,
the third side of your universe.
                        add on
Alice Coltrane and her cosmic strains, still no
       vocal
on blue-black horizons / your plasticity is tested
by a formless assault: THE SUN can answer
       questions
in tune to sacrificial silence / but why will our
new jazz age give us no more expanding puzzles?
       (Enter John) blow from under always and
          never so that,
the morning may shout of brain-
bending saxophones.

       the third world arrives with Yusef Lateef
and
Pharoah Sanders with oboes straining to touch the
core of your unknown soul.
       Ravi Shankar comes
       with strings attached / prepared to stabilize
       your seventh sense (Black Rhythm!)
up and down a silly ladder run the notes without
the words. words are important for the mind / the
notes are for the soul.

                    Miles Davis? SO WHAT?
                 Cannonball / Fiddler / Mercy
              Dexter Gordon/ONE flight UP
           Donald Byrd / Cristo
                             but what about words?
        would you like to survive on sadness /call on
              Ella and Jose Happiness /

                                    drift with

        Smoky / Bill Medley / Bobby Taylor /
        Otis / soul music where frustrations are
        washed by drums—come Nina and Miriam—
        congo / mongo beat me senseless
        bongo / tonto—flash through dream worlds of
              STP and LSD. SpEeD kilLs and
          some—/—times
        music's call to the Black is confused. our
        speed is our life pace / not safe / not good.
        i beg you to escape
              and live
                 and hear all of the real. to survive in a
                 sincere second of self-self
        until a call comes for you to cry elsewhere.

                                         we

              must all cry, but must the tears be white?

The Revolution Will Not Be Televised

You will not be able to stay home, brother.
You will not be able to plug in, turn on and cop
out.
You will not be able to lose yourself on scag and
skip out for beer during commercials because
The revolution will not be televised.

The revolution will not be televised.
The revolution will not be brought to you
by Xerox in four parts without commercial
interruption.
The revolution will not show you pictures of
Nixon blowing a bugle and leading a charge by
John Mitchell, General Abramson and Spiro
Agnew to eat hog maws confiscated from a
Harlem sanctuary.
The revolution will not be televised.

The revolution will not be brought to you by
The Schaeffer Award Theatre and will not star
Natalie Wood and Steve McQueen or Bullwinkle
and Julia.
The revolution will not give your mouth sex
appeal.
The revolution will not get rid of the nubs.
The revolution will not make you look five
pounds thinner.
The revolution will not be televised, brother.

There will be no pictures of you and Willie Mae
pushing that shopping cart down the block on
the dead run
or trying to slide that color t.v. in a stolen
ambulance.
NBC will not be able to predict the winner at

8:32 on reports from twenty-nine districts.
The revolution will not be televised.

There will be no pictures of pigs shooting down
  brothers
on the instant replay.
There will be no pictures of pigs shooting down
  brothers
on the instant replay.
The will be no slow motion or still lifes of Roy
  Wilkins strolling through Watts in a red, black
  and green liberation jumpsuit that he has been
  saving for just the proper occasion.

Green Acres, Beverly Hillbillies and Hooterville
  Junction
will no longer be so damned relevant
and women will not care if Dick finally got down
  with Jane
on Search for Tomorrow
because black people will be in the streets
  looking for
A Brighter Day.
The revolution will not be televised.

There will be no highlights on the Eleven
  O'Clock News
and no pictures of hairy armed women
  liberationists
and Jackie Onassis blowing her nose.
The theme song will not be written by Jim
  Webb or Francis Scott Key
nor sung by Glen Campbell, Tom Jones, Johnny
  Cash,
Englebert Humperdink or Rare Earth.
The revolution will not be televised.

The revolution will not be right back after a
message about a white tornado, white lightning
   or white people.
You will not have to worry about a dove in your
   bedroom,
the tiger in your tank or the giant in your toilet
   bowl.
The revolution will not go better with coke.
The revolution will not fight germs that may
   cause bad breath.
The revolution *will* put you in the driver's seat.
The revolution will not be televised
                    will not be televised
                        not be televised
                           be televised
The revolution will be no re-run, brothers.
The revolution will be LIVE.

H₂O Gate Blues

Click! Whirr...Click!
"I'm sorry, the government you have elected is
    inoperative...
Click! Inoperative!"
Just how blind will America be?
The world is on the edge of its seat
defeat on the horizon, very surprisin'
that we all could see the plot
and claimed that we could not.
Just how blind, America?
Just how blind, Americans?
Just as Viet Nam exploded in the rice
snap, crackle and pop
could not stop people determined to be free.
The shock of a Viet Nam defeat
sent Republican donkeys scurrying down on
    Wall Street
and when the roll was called it was:
Phillips 66 and Pepsi-Cola plastics,
Boeing Dow and Lockheed—
ask them what we're fighting for
and they never mention the economics of war.
Ecological Warfare! Above all else destroy the
    land!
If we can't break the Asian's will
We'll bomb the dykes and starve the man!

America! The international Jekyll and Hyde,
the land of a thousand disguises
sneaks up but rarely surprises,
plundering the Asian countryside in the name of
    Fu Man Chu.
Just how long, America?
Just how long, Americans?
Who was around where Hale Boggs died

and what about LBJ's untimely demise?
And whatever happened to J. Edgar Hoover?
The king is proud of Patrick Gray
while America's faith is drowning
   beneath that cesspool—Watergate.

How long will the citizens sit and wait?
It's looking like Europe in '38 and
did they move to stop Hitler before it was too
   late?
How long, America before the consequences of:
allowing the press to be intimidated
keeping the school system segregated
watching the price of everything soar
and hearing complaints 'cause the rich want
   more?
It seems that MacBeth, and not his lady, went
   mad.
We've let him eliminate the whole middle class.
What really happened to J. Edgar Hoover?
The king is proud of Patrick Gray
while America's faith is drowning
beneath that cesspool—Watergate.
How much more evidence do the citizens need
that the election was rigged with trickery and
   greed?
And, if this is so, and who we got didn't win
let's do the whole Goddam election over again!
The obvious key to the whole charade
would be to run down all the games that they
   played:
Remember Dita Beard and ITT, the slaughter of
   Attica,
the C.I.A. in Chile knowing nothing about
   Allende at this time
in the past. The slaughter in Augusta, G.A.
the nomination of Supreme Court Jesters to
   head off the tapes,

William Calley's Executive Interference in the
image of John Wayne,
Kent State, Jackson State, Southern Louisiana,
Hundreds of unauthorized bombing raids,
the chaining and gagging of Bobby Seale—
somebody tell these jive Maryland Governors to
    be for real!
We recall all of these events just to prove
that Waterbuggers in the Watergate wasn't no
    news!
And the thing that justifies all our fears
is that all this went down in the last five years.
And what really happened to J. Edgar Hoover?
The king is proud of Patrick Gray
while America's faith is drowning
beneath that cesspool—Watergate.

We leave America to ponder the image of its
    new leadership:
Frank Rizzo, the high school graduate Mayor of
    Philadelphia, whose
ignorance is surpassed only by those who voted
    for him.
Richard Daley, Mayor of Chicago, who took
    over from Al Capone and
continues to implement the same tactics.
Lester Maddawg, George Wallace, Strom
    Thurmond, Ronald Reagan—
an almost endless list that won't be missed
    when at last
America is purged.
And the silent White House with the James
    Brothers once in command.
Sauerkraut Mafia men deserting the sinking
    White House ship and
their mindless, meglomaniac Ahab.
McCord has blown. Mitchell has blown.
No tap on my telephone.

51

Haldeman, Erlichmann, Mitchell and Dean
It follows a pattern if you dig what I mean.
And what are we left with?
Bumper stickers saying Free the Watergate 500,
spy movies of the same name with a cast of
   thousands,
and that ominous phrase: If Nixon knew, Agnew!
What really happened to J. Edgar Hoover?
The king is proud of Patrick Gray
while America's faith is drowning
beneath that cesspool—Watergate.

Beginnings
(The First Minute of a New Day)

We're sliding through completely new
beginnings.
We're searching out our every doubt
and winning.
We want to be free
and yet we have no idea
why we are struggling here
faced with our every fear
just to survive.

We've heard the sound and come around
to listening.
We've touched the vibes time after time
insisting that we know what life means;
still we can't break away
from dues we've got to pay
we hope will somehow say
that we're alive.

We Beg Your Pardon, America

We beg your pardon, America.
We beg your pardon
because the pardon you gave this time
was not yours to give.
They call it due process and some people are
    overdue.
We beg your pardon, America.
Somebody said "BrotherMan gon' break a
    window,
gon' steal a hub cap,
gon' smoke a joint and BrotherMan gon' go to
    jail."
The man who tried to steal America is not in
    jail.
Get caught with a nickel bag, BrotherMan!
Get caught with a nickel bag, SisterLady
on your way to get yo' hair fixed!
You'll do Big Ben and Big Ben is Time.
A man who tried to fix America will not do
    time.
Said they wuz gonna' slap his wrist
and retire him with $850,000.
America was shocked!
America leads the world in shock.
Unfortunately, America doesn't lead the world
in deciphering
the cause of shock.
Eight hundred and fifty thousand dollars they
said and the people protested;
so they said, "All right, we'll give him $200,000."
Everybody said, "Okay, that's better."
I'd like to retire with $200,000 some day.
San Quentin, not San Clemente!
Go directly to jail, Do not pass Go! Do not
    collect $200,000.

We beg your pardon, America
We beg your pardon
because somehow the pardon did not sit
    correctly,
What were the causes for this pardon?
Well, they had phlebitis.
Rats bite us — no pardon in the ghetto.
They said National Security, but do you feel
    secure
with the man who tried to steal America
back on the streets again?
And what were the results of this pardon?
We now have Oatmeal Man.

Anytime you find someone in the middle
Anytime you find someone who is lukewarm
Anytime you find someone
who has been in Congress for twenty-five years
and no one ever heard of him, you've got
    Oatmeal Man.
Oatmeal Man: straddling uncomfortably
yards of barbed wire.
Oatmeal Man: The man who said
you could fit all of his Black friends
in the trunk of his car and still have room
for the Republican elephant.
Oatmeal Man: There was no crime he
    committed.
Oatmeal Man says that, America,
In 1975 your President will
be a 1913 Ford.
Regressive.
Circle up the wagons
to defend
yourself from nuclear attack.
Reminiscent of 1964's Goldwater.
Thank God he didn't win.
But Oatmeal Man didn't win.

I didn't vote for him.
Did you vote for him?

But that's the first result. And the second would
    be:
The dread Rockefeller. Doubtlessly being
    promoted
for the job he did at Attica.
Forty-three dead and millions of Americans
Once again, in shock!
Doubtlessly being promoted for the job he did
    on the streets
of New York City, where the pushers push
    drugs that the
government allows in the country to further
    suppress the masses
who then do time.
They do life or death or life and death
behind bars.
While William Saxbe wanted to dismiss
the Lorton Furlough Program
and Brother Richard X faces 1,365 years
(did he say one thousand three hundred and
    sixty-five years) for participating at Attica.
Rockefeller faces the Vice-Presidency of this
    country
for his participation.
And all is calm and quiet
along the white sands at San Clemente.

We beg your pardon, America.
We beg your pardon, once again
because we found that seven out of every
    ten Black men
are behind bars
(and it seems that seven out of every ten men
    behind bars are Black)
seven out of every ten of these Black men

never went to the 9th grade
and hadn't had a hundred dollars for a month
when they went to jail.
So the poor and the ignorant go to jail
while the rich go to San Clemente.
We beg your pardon, America
because we understand much better than we
    understood before.
But we don't want you to take the pardon back.
We want you to issue some more.
Pardon Brother Frank Willis, the Watergate
    security guard.
He was only doing his job (and now he can't
    find one).
Pardon H. Rap Brown, it was only burglary.
Pardon Robert Vesco, it was only embezzlement.
And pardon us while we get sick.
Because they pardoned William Calley:
twenty two dead and America in shock.
And as we understand all the better, we beg your
    pardon
as unemployment spirals to seven per cent
(and it seems like seventy per cent in my
    neighborhood)
as we watch cattlemen on TV shoot cows in the
    head
and kick them into graves
while millions are starving in the Sahel
and Honduras and maybe even next door.
We understand all the more deeply
as Boston becomes Birmingham becomes Little
    Rock becomes Selma, becomes Philadelphia,
        Mississippi
becomes yesterday all over again.
We understand and we beg your pardon.
We beg your pardon, America
because we have an understanding of karma:
what goes around comes around.

We beg your pardon, America
because the pardon you gave this time was not
yours to give.

The Ghetto Code
(DOT-DOT-DIT-DIT-DOT-DOT-DASH)

Communication has always been an important part of our existence. In Africa we were dependent upon the drummer's rhythm to keep us informed and in touch with villages far up the Nile. As captives, in this country, our contact through the drums was destroyed, but not our need to communicate or our need for independent communications.

For the past couple of years, we have seen a totally new Ghetto Code begin to develop. The primary phrase that has caught on from the code has been "Dot-dot-dit-dit-dot-dot-dash." It means "Damned if I know." Daily there are more and more revelations that make us uncertain of things we thought we were positive about. So: "Dot-dot-dit-dit-dot-dot-dash." Damned if I know.

A good example I might give would be Astrology. Lately, more and more people have been re-investigating Astrology — finding out what their signs and their placements are. That was all well and good until folks found out that somebody had been messing with the calendar. They found out that the month in our calendar called July was slipped in to honor Julius Caesar. They found the month called August had been slipped in to honor Augustus Caesar. They found there was a problem with September because it is the Latin word for *seventh*, but it is the *ninth* month in our calendar. And people familiar with the romance languages jumped all over it — octo means eight, but October is the *tenth* month; nove means nine, but November is *eleventh*; and dece means ten, but December is *twelfth*! "Dot-dot-dit-dit-dot-dot-dash." Damned if I know.

The problem seems to originate in February. It takes at least thirty days to qualify as a month (the precedent having been established by the other eleven). Yet, February has twenty-eight days three times in a row and if you make the leap year, you get a bonus. "Dot-dot-dit-dit-dot-dot-dash." Damned if I know.

There was another problem with the alphabet. Tracing the origins of the symbols, I found that they were called "Alpha Beta" and contained *all* of these symbols from Alpha to Omega — that is from beginning to end. From Alpha — the letter a — the beginning, to Omega — the letter q — the end; but they got nine more letters coming after "the end." R-S-T-U-V-W-X-Y-Z. What do I think? "Dot dot-dit-dit-dot-dot-dash." Damned if I know!

The letter that has become my favorite is the letter "c." It is multipurpose, but it does not receive the proper amount of respect. Highly underrated.

The first letter in Cash.
The first letter in Constitution.
The last letter in musiC.
The first letter in C.I.A.
The C.I.A. and F.B.I., noses pressed against our
    windowpanes,
Ears glued to our telephone.
Why won't they leave us alone?
Trying to pick up on...the Ghetto Code.

Old fashioned Ghetto codes saw phone
    conversations like this:
"Hey, Bree-is-other me-is-an? You goin' to the
    pe-is-arty to ne-is-ite?"
Oh, yeah! Well, why not bring me a nee-is-ickel
    be-is-ag? You dig?"
I know who ever they was paying at the time to
listen in on my calls had to be scratchin' his head
sayin', "Dot-dot-dit-dit-dot-dot-dash." (Damned if
I know!)

But as to the letter "c." If it reminds you of cash money, there is a definite connection. The C.I.A. was responsible for the transfer of $400,000,000 to one Howard Hughes. This $400,000,000 (give or take a million or two) was to be used for a covert salvaging mission at sea, to be undertaken by a Hughes seacraft, the Glo-Mar Challenger. This salvage craft would be used to recover a Russian submarine that sank in 1968. The reason the recovery of this submarine was *so* important to our government was because of the Russian codes on board.

The Russian sub had allegedly broken into three pieces somewhere in the Pacific (which is almost like saying somewhere on the planet Earth). The Glo-Mar located the sub and proceeded to salvage it with, we believe, a giant magnet.

The magnet went down and recovered the first third of the Russian sub, containing some seventy dead Russian sailors. (No advantage there. Considering the sizeable sum allocated and the zero rubles put forth by the Kremlin.) The second part of the sub to be brought to the surface had two Polaris-styled nuclear warheads on board. (No real advantage there. This country has already stockpiled sufficient nuclear weapons to have damn near one bomb for every individual. These recovered Russian weapons could not have made the $400 million difference.) Then comes the strange part of the operation. As preparations were being made to recover the third and final part, the part with the all-important code books on board, questions began to bubble to the surface.

"The Russian sub went in 1968, right?"
"We've been trying to find those code books for almost six years now, right?"
"When you lose your code books, don't you change your codes?"
"If they've changed their codes, why did we spend all that money?" "Dot-dot-dit-dit-dot-dot-dash."
(Damned if I know.)

But perhaps your personal problems do not revolve around cash. Perhaps the "c" will remind you of Cuba. There was a C.I.A. coordinated invasion of Cuba at the Bay of Pigs. The invasion was a total failure, but it did reveal clues that had to do with an assassination attempt on a man whose name starts with "c" — Castro.

The "c" might remind you of Chile. Over eight million American dollars were spent there by the C.I.A. to help overthrow and destroy a man named Salvador Allende who just happened to be a "c" — communist.

The "c" might remind you of the Canal. The Panama Canal. The covert base established in Panama by the C.I.A. to institute plans for "c" — Columbia eventually led to the destruction of "c" — Che Guevara.

The "c" might remind you of the Congo. The Belgian Congo. Before Zaire was there, there were revolutionary factions brooding in Katanga province. In 1960, there was a statement from a Black leader indicating the possible requeste d'intervention from the Soviet Union shortly before a coup d'etat that left him dead of assassination. His name? Patrice Lumumba.

A string of questions with few answers. Problems with few solutions like: "Was that Lee Harvey Oswald over there? Or in that corner? Was he 5'8", 165 pounds or 6'2", 205? Was he photographed for his passport in Dallas or was that Moscow?

Arthur Bremmer. Was he from Massachusetts, Michigan or Maryland? Was he captured in the midwest or the Middle East? And if they always have a photo of them before they commit these crimes, why can't they stop them?" "Dot-dot-dit-dit-dot-dot-dash." (Damned if I know.)

There seems to have been a stream of too many unanswered questions that always had tracks leading back to the same doorway.

JFK. You believe that?
RFK. You believe that?
MLK. You believe that?
Malcolm X. You believe that?
All some elaborate "c" — Coincidence?
Or just a little old "c" — Conspiracy?

There are several questions concerning the letter
"c," this most important of letters, that most in-
dividuals should be asking themselves:
"The C.I.A...who runs that organization?"
And, "Who runs this country?"
"Dot-dot-dit-dit-dot-dot-dash." (Damned if I know!)

Bicentennial Blues

Some people think that America invented the
 blues
and few people doubt that America is the home
 of the blues.
And the bluesicians have gone all over the world
 carrying the
blues message and the world has snapped its
 fingers and tapped
its feet right along with the blues folks, but
the blues has always been totally American.
As American as apple pie.
As American as the blues.
As American as apple pie.
The question is why...
why should the blues
 be so at home here?
Well, America provided the atmosphere
America provided the atmosphere for the blues
and the blues was born.
The blues was born on the American wilderness,
The blues was born on the beaches where the
 slave ships docked,
born on the slave man's auction block
The blues was born and carried on the howling
 wind.
The blues grew up a slave,
The blues grew up as property.
The blues grew up in Nat Turner visions.
The blues grew up in Harriet Tubman courage.
The blues grew up in small town deprivation.
The blues grew up in the nightmares of the
 white man.
The blues grew up in the blues singing of
Bessie and Billie and Ma.
The blues grew up in Satchmo's horn, on Duke's

piano
in Langston's poetry, on Robeson's baritone.
The point is...that the blues is grown.
The blues is grown now—fully grown and you
   can trace/
the evolution of the blues on a parallel line
with the evolution of this country.
From Plymouth Rock to acid rock.
From 13 states to Watergate,
The blues is grown, but not the home.
The blues is grown, but the country has not.
The blues remembers everything the country
   forgot.

It's a Bicentennial year and the blues is
celebrating a birthday, and it's a Bicentennial
   blues.
America has got the blues and it's a Bicentennial
   edition.
The blues view may amuse you but make
no mistake—it's a Bicentennial year.
A year of hysterical importance
A year of historical importance:
ripped-off like donated moments
from the past.
Two hundred years ago this evening.
Two hundred years ago last evening, and what
   about now?
The blues is now.
The blues has grown up and the country has not.
The country has been ripped-off!
Ripped-off like the Indians!
Ripped-off like jazz!
Ripped-off like nature!
Ripped-off like Christmas!
Manhandled by media over-kill,
Goosed by aspiring Vice Presidents.
Violated by commercial corporations—A

Bicentennial year
The year the symbol transformed into the B-U-Y-
    centennial.
Buy a car.
Buy a flag.
Buy a map...until the public en masse has been
    bludgeoned into
Bicentennial submission
or Bicentennial suspicion.
I fall into the latter category...
It's a blues year and America
has got the blues.
It's got the blues because of
partial deification of
partial accomplishments over a
partial period of time.
Half-way justice.
Half-way liberty.
Half-way equality.
It's a half-ass year
and we would be silly in all our knowledge,
in all our self-righteous knowledge
When we sit back and laugh and mock the
    things
that happen in our lives;
to accept anything less than the truth
about this Bicentennial year.

And the truth relates to two hundred years of
people and ideas getting by!
It got by George Washington!
The ideas of justice, liberty and equality got cold
by George Washington.
Slave owner general!
Ironic that the father of this country
should be a slave owner.
The father of this country a slave owner
having got by him

it made it easy to get by his henchmen,
the creators of this liberty,
who slept in bed with the captains of the slave
    ships,
Fought alongside Black freed men in the Union
    Army,
and left America a legacy of hypocrisy.
It's blues year.
Got by Gerald Ford!

Oatmeal Man.
Has declared himself at odds with people
on welfare...people who get food stamps,
day care children, the elderly, the poor, women
    and
people who might vote for Ronald Reagan.
Ronald Reagan—It got by him. Hollyweird!
Acted like an actor
acted like a liberal
acted like General Franco, when he acted like
Governor of California.
Now he acts like somebody might vote for him
    for President.
It got by Jimmy Carter,
"Skippy."
Got by Jimmy Carter and got by him and his
    friend
the Colonel...the creators of southern fried
    triple talk,
A blues trio.
America got the blues.
It got by Henry Kissinger
the international Godfather of peace.
A Piece of Vietnam!
A Piece of Laos!
A Piece of Angola!
A Piece of Cuba!

A blues quartet and America got the blues.
The point is that it may get by you
for another four years
for another eight years...you stuck playing
   second fiddle
in a blues quartet.
Got the bues looking for the first principle
which was justice.
It's a blues year for justice.
It's a blues year for the San Quentin Six, looking
   for
justice.
It's a blues year for Gary Tyler, looking for justice.
It's a blues year for Rev. Ben Chavis, looking for
   justice.
It's a blues year for Boston, looking for justice.
It's a blues year for babies
on buses,
It's a blues year for mothers and fathers with
   babies on buses.
It's a blues year for Boston and it's a blues year
all over this country.
America has got the blues and the blues is
in the street looking for three principles—
justice, liberty, equality
We would do well to join the blues looking for
justice, liberty, and equality.
The blues is in the street.
America has got the blues but don't let it get by
us.

The New Deal

I have believed in my convictions
and been convicted for my beliefs.
I have been conned by the Constitution
and harassed by the police.
I have been billed for the Bill of Rights
as though I'd done something wrong.
I have become a special amendment
for what included me all along.
Like: "All men are created equal."
(No amendment needed there)
I've contributed in every field including cotton
from Sunset Strip to Washington Square.
Back during the non-violent era
I was the only non-violent one.
Come to think of it there was no non-violence
'cause too many rednecks had guns.
There seems to have been this pattern
that took a long time to pick up on.
But all black leaders who dared stand up
wuz in jail, in the courtroom or gone.
Picked up indiscriminately
by the shocktroops of discrimination
to end up in jails or tied up in trials
while dirty tricks soured the nation.
I've been hoodwinked by professional hoods,
My ego had happened to me.
"Just keep things cool!" they kept repeating.
"And keep the people out of the streets.
We'll settle all this at the conference table.
You leave everything to me."
Which brings me back to my convictions
and being convicted for my beliefs
'cause I believe these smiles
in three piece suits
with gracious, liberal demeanor

took our movement off the streets
and took us to the cleaners.
In other words, we let up the pressure
and that was all part of their plan
and every day we allow to slip through our fingers
is playing right into their hands.

A Poem for Jose Campos Torres

I had said I wasn't gonna' write no more poems
    like this.
I had confessed to myself all along, tracer of
    life/poetry trends,
that awareness/consciousness poems that screamed
    of pain
and the origins of pain and death had blanketed
    my tablets and therefore
my friends/brothers/sisters/outlaws/in-laws
and besides, they already knew.
But brother Torres,
common, ancient bloodline brother Torres,
is dead.
I had said I wasn't gonna write no more poems
    like this.
I had said I wasn't gonna write no more words
    down
about people kickin' us when we're down
about racist dogs that attack us and
drive us down, drag us down and beat us down.
But the dogs are in the street!
The dogs are alive and the terror in our hearts
    has scarcely diminished.
It has scarcely brought us the comfort we
    suspected:
the recognition of our terror,
and the screaming release of that recognition
has not removed the certainty of that
    knowledge.
How could it?
The dogs, rabid, foaming with the energy of their
    brutish ignorance,
stride the city streets like robot gunslingers, and
    spread death

as night lamps flash crude reflections from gun
   butts and police shields.

I had said I wasn't gonna' write no more poems
   like this.
But the battle field has oozed away from the
   stilted debates of
semantics, beyond the questionable flexibility of
   primal screaming.
The reality of our city/jungle streets and their
   gestapos has
become an attack on home/life/family/
   philosophy/total.
It is beyond a question of the advantages of
   didactic niggerisms.
The MOTHERFUCKIN' DOGS are in the street!
In Houston maybe someone said Mexicans were
   the new niggers.
In L.A. maybe someone decided Chicanos were
   the new niggers.
In Frisco maybe someone said Asians were the
   new niggers.
Maybe in Philadelphia and North Carolina they
   decided they
didn't need no new niggers.

I had said I wasn't gonna' write no more poems
   like this.
But the dogs are in the street.
It's a turn around world where things all too
   quickly turn around.
It was turned around so that right looked wrong.
It was turned around so that up looked down.
It was turned around so that those who marched
   in the streets
with Bibles and signs of peace became enemies
   of the state
and risks to National Security;

So that those who questioned the operations of
  those in authority
on the principles of justice, liberty, and equality
  became the vanguard of a communist attack.
It became so you couldn't call a spade a
  motherfuckin' spade.
Brother Torres is dead.
The Wilmington Ten are still incarcerated.
Ed Davis, Ronald Regan and James Hunt and
  Frank Rizzo are still alive.
And the dogs are in the MOTHERFUCKIN' street.
I had said I wasn't gonna' write no more poems
  like this.
I made a mistake.

Afterword

Gil Scott-Heron: Larry Neal's Quintessential Artist

Dr. Joyce Joyce

In the afterword to *Black Fire*, the invaluable anthology of Black American literature, edited by Larry Neal and LeRoi Jones (Amiri Baraka), Larry Neal presents in general terms his ideas concerning the responsibility of the Black writer and his search for form. He asserts, "Black literature must become an integral part of the community's life-style. And I believe that it must also be integral to the myths and experiences underlying the total history of black people."[1] Thus, Neal denounces the traditional attitude that separates the literary artist and his works from society's common masses. The Black writer's responsibility is to use literature to "move people to a deeper understanding"[2] of their lives and of the forces that manipulate their lives. Consequently, instead of echoing the rhythms and ideologies of a Western literary tradition that attempts to strip the Black man of his humanity and ignore that part of his culture which makes him unique, the Black artist must look to his unique history and to his people for the ideas and techniques for shaping his art. Neal writes:

> ... the key to where black people have to go is in the music. Our music has always been the most dominant manifestation of what we are and feel; literature was just an afterthought, the step taken by the Negro bourgeoisie who desired acceptance in the white man's terms. And that is precisely why the literature has failed. It was the case of one elite addressing another elite. But our music is something else. The best of it has always operated at the core of our lives, forcing itself

upon us as in a ritual. It has always, somehow, represented the collective psyche.[3]

Neal proposes, then, that the Black American musician is the artist of the people. He embodies the ideas of the people, and it is he who has always been faithful to his role in furthering the "psychological liberation of his people."[4] Gil Scott-Heron — a poet, a novelist, a political activist, a composer, and a musician — is the quintessential example of what Neal believes the Black artist should be. He is the "priest" or Black magician who makes "juju with the word on the *world*."[5] His music represents Black people's "collective psyche." Scott-Heron, like Neal, recognizes the need to take the message to the people. And the people, those Black folk we call the grass roots, do not search the novel for meaning in their lives nor for solace of their suffering. The music of Black folk has always been the magnifying glass that illuminated the traditions and struggles of Black people. Thus music is the quintessential medium through which the artist can liberate the Black masses. Scott-Heron's lyrics and rhythms move people to a deeper understanding of what their lives are about. From his successful collector's album *Pieces of a Man* to *Moving Target (1982)*, he writes to and about the people as well as performs for the people.

Scott-Heron's works reveal his consistent denunciation of the meretricious beauties that embody a capitalistic society, his consistent concern with those stifling aspects of our society from which young Blacks seek solace in drugs, his consistent remonstration of an American prison system that has a predominately Black population, and his consistent attempt to make Black people more aware of the political forces that shape and manipulate their lives. Although *Moving Target* has an up-beat rhythm-and-blues base line distinctly different from the heavy, slow blues quality of *Winter in America*, one of his most popular earlier albums, his works are aesthetically poetic and beautifully musical renderings of Black cultural and political history.

I divide Scott-Heron's song into five interrelated modes: the poetic-blues rap (or the satiric monologue), the people's folktale, the musical poem, the mellow lyric, and the satirical lyric. "The Revolution Will Not Be Televised," "H2O Gate Blues," "Bicentennial Blues," and the even more humorous "The Ghetto Code (Dot-Dot-Dit-Dit-Dot-Dot-Dash)" are four of his most well-known raps. A modern-day paradigm with the same rap as Shine from the well-known folktale or an educated, intellectual version of the Black man who stands in front of the Dew Drop Inn, Scott-Heron often begins his concerns with a clever and humorous monologue designed to entertain, inspire, and enlighten. During these raps, he refers to himself as a "bluesician." He defines the term in "Bicentennial Blues," explaining that the blues is totally American, "as American as Apple Pie." America, he continues, provided the atmosphere for the blues. "The blues was born in the American wilderness, on the beaches where the slave ships docked. The blues grew up a slave; the blues grew up as poverty, in Nat-Turner visions, in big-city isolation, in the blues singing of Bessie, Billie, Moms, Robeson, and Satchmo's horn." He adds, "Blues has grown, but the country has not." This monologue of "rap," taken from his 1976 recording *It's Your World*, poetically and implicitly explains that a bluesician is a musician whose art addresses the suffering and history of Black Americans.

In defining "the means and modes" associated with the blues, "Bicentennial Blues" meshes the folk and political history of Black Americans with an attack on the evils of commercialism. Scott-Heron's "means" here illuminates the unique quality of a style that echoes the humorous sounds of a Black community: 1976 is a year of "hysterical importance" and a year of "historical importance" in which Black people are "Bogarted into bicentennial submission or bicentennial suspicion." Playing on the sounds of these words, Scott-Heron admonishes Black Americans to become suspicious of "media overkill," to be aware of the pitfalls of a history that should have taught them the evils of the "b-u-y syndrome." This timely album cautions Black people to be mindful of their economic-exploitative history in relationship to the dominant American culture. The pun on the prefix "bi" in "Bicentennial Blues" exemplifies his satiric use of a title to introduce the meaning of his songs. Other representative "raps" include the humorous, satirical "H2O Gate Blues" — which explores the political realities of the Watergate incident — and the superb definition of the Ghetto Code in "Dot-Dot-Dit-Dit-Dot-Dot-Dash" found on *The Mind of Gil Scott-Heron: A Collection of His Poetry and Music* (Arista Records, 1979).

Although all of Scott-Heron's songs embody characteristics from all the five categories into which I divide his work, overriding characteristics in each group justify such categorization. "Possum Slim" from *It's Your World* (1976), "Under the Hammer" from *Bridges* (1977), and "Three Miles Down" from *Secrets* (1978) all represent what I refer to as the people's folktale because they chant of the suffering embodied in the daily lives of the Black masses. Because of its sparse narrative line characteristic of the Black folktale, "Possum Slim" best exemplifies this second group. Of course, the title itself indicates that the subject of the song comes from the Black masses. For the name Possum Slim, like Pigmeat and Moms Mabley, results from a tradition in which Black people in America separated from their African heritage were forced to create their own customs. Hence, many of the names in the Black community reflect the history of a displaced people who forged a heritage out of their folk customs. "Possum Slim" is the story of a 105-year-old brother who is in a Florida jail. First we learn that we are not to "mess with" Possum Slim. By beginning this way, Scott-Heron paints a picture of a stereotypical bad dude. But next we hear that Possum Slim (this man whom we are told in a refrain is over a hundred years old) was beaten up and robbed by his friends or people whom he thought were his friends. This Black old man who has eked out his existence for over a hundred years is abused by his Black brothers who should respect the time that he has had to cultivate his relationship to the earth. Outraged and hurt, Possum Slim took all he could. But "Robbed so many times/I reckon he couldn't take no more," he responded with violence because his "friends" tried to take a five-dollar bill while Possum Slim was on his way to a birthday party for a woman he "knowed." Scott-Heron explains, "Brother took all he could/story don't prove that he ain't no good." We are not supposed to judge Possum Slim; instead we are supposed to understand him as the sun does: "Sun knowed Possum Slim for a 100 years/Sun can't help but smile." The sun, a natural heavenly force, understands that Possum Slim acted very naturally. He weathered the hostile forces that attempted to subdue him until his nature demanded that he act. The five-dollar bill indicates both Possum Slim's poverty and the lack of integrity and total corruption of those "brothers" who would steal five dollars from a hundred-and-five-year-old man. This song, then, a true folktale of the people, emphasizes the moral degradation of people trapped inside a racist culture.

Akin to his people's folktale is the musical poem. For Gil Scott-Heron's skill at poetry manifests the rhythms and feelings peculiar to a Black tradition; yet some of his songs are so heavily poetic that I call them musical poems. All of the songs from his unusual recording entitled *1980* fall into this category. Because of this timely reference to the Iranian crisis and its sustained metaphor, the song "Shah Mot (The Shah is Dead/Checkmate)" best represents this album. Again characteristic of Scott-Heron's technique, the title adds to the meaning and reflects the style of the song. As with "bi" in "Bicentennial Blues," Scott-Heron plays on the sound of "Shah Mot," which more than vaguely echoes "checkmate." This song beautifully shows that Scott-Heron is as much of a political activist as he is a musician-poet. The etymology of "checkmate" reveals the Arabic origin "shah mot" which means "the king is perplexed or dead." Hence, the subtitle of Scott-Heron's poem: "The Shah is Dead/Checkmate." Checkmate is, of course, the signal in a chess game that the king has been captured and the game won by the king's opponent. The double sound of the title "Shah Mot" then reflects the double meaning sustained throughout the poem. The song figuratively, never explicitly, refers to two kings: the Shah and Carter. Scott-Heron uses chess, a political game modeled on war, to represent metaphorically the political relationship between the Shah and Carter and the oppressed Iranians and oppressed Black Americans.

Like the king on a chess board, the president or king of a nation maintains a most important and most vulnerable position. Scott-Heron's poem shows that both kings—the Shah and Carter—lost their power. In the first stanza, he addresses the affinity between the Iranians and Black Americans by the figurative double meaning suggested in the title and continued throughout the poem:

My name is What's your name/ I am the voice of same;
Remembering things that I told me yesterday.
My name is What's your name/ I am inside your frame;
We knew the devils, had to make them go away.
My name is What's your name/ You might reject my claim,
I expect that you won't vary from the norm.
My name is What's your name/ Ours is a single aim
And we can double recognize the needed form:
Take it to the streets!
Tell everybody you meet!
Do whatever you do whenever you hear the war drums beat.
Put it in the air!
Spread it everywhere!
Do whatever you do whenever you know you've go to be there.
Shah Mot! You only take it as a symbol.
Shah Mot! Look closely: who does it resemble?

This beautiful stanza alludes to the interrelationship between the Iranians and Black Americans. These two groups are "the voice of same." The things the "I" remembers make up the history of Black Americans. "I am inside your frame" refers to the commonality of the physiological and geographical origins of the Iranians and Black Americans. The "devils," of course, alludes to the white man whose influence the Iranian students "had to make go away." The goal of the oppressed Black American and that of the Iranian people should have "a single aim." If the Iranians — who are double oppressed by the Shah and by whites — unite with Black Americans ideologically, these two groups can "double recognize the needed form." In other words, they can strengthen their physical, emotional, and ideological forces. The colon after "form" indicates that what follows is an explanation of the form, an indication of what should be the notions of these groups. The message, the "it" in the poem, is the word that expresses the shared historical and ideological similarities and the need for awareness on the part of both the Iranians and Black Americans. The line "Do whatever you do whenever you hear the war drums beat" emphasizes a need for action induced by the sound of war drums (or by the feelings evoked by Scott-Heron's music). The last two lines of this stanza sum up and reiterate the relationship between the two oppressed groups. We only take "Shah Mot!" as a symbol for a play used in a chess game (checkmate) or as a phrase that in part echoes the name for the title of the leader of Iran, but if we look closely, we shall see that the history and political dilemma of the Iranian people closely resemble the experiences of Black Americans. This poetic song, more so than any of the others, sanctions Scott-Heron as the purest example of Neal's main criteria for the Black artist. Like Scott-Heron, "the Black artist and the political activist are one."[6]

Following the traditional definition of a lyric, I choose to put the mellow lyric in its own category separate from the musical poem. Usually on each of his albums, Scott-Heron includes a song about the self. We can identify this self with Scott-Heron, or we can be a bit traditional and say that he gives us a persona who sings in these "mellow lyrics" of his desire to assuage the sufferings of his brothers, of the loneliness and frustration of being a musician, and of love. In "Song of the Wind" from *Bridges* (1977), Scott-Heron echoes the nineteenth-century English Romantic poet Percy Bysshe Shelley's famous "Ode to the West Wind." In this poem Shelley, who sees himself as a kind of prophet, asks the wind to carry his thoughts (his words) to mankind just as it drives the leaves, moves seeds, loosens the clouds, and awakens the waves of the blue Mediterranean. In "Song of the Wind," Scott-Heron directly uses the wind as a metaphor for the poet's word:

Blow wind blow/ Further than a thousand wires.
Blow wind blow/ Transporter of the clouds.
Blow wind blow/ Fanner of a thousand fires.
Can't you see that every place you go
The people got a need to understand,
People want to know
Won't you blow wind, blow?

He sings with a steady, relaxed voice. Accompanying a soft drum beat, piano and subtle bongoes is the sound of birds chirping in the background. Even at the end of the song when he becomes most subjective and prophetic, the melody and his voice remain soft and unobtrusive. In this last verse, he asserts that the poet has the vision needed to use the past to presage the future and that the poet's duty is to help his people:

Blow wind blow/ Tell them don't give up the fight.
Blow wind blow/ Through the calm and through the storm.
Blow wind blow/ Through the pages of my life.
Can't you see traveling on the wings of time
That only you can look ahead (and see what's happenin')
As clearly as you see behind
Won't you blow wind blow?

The differences between "Song of the Wind" and "A Legend in His Own Mind" beautifully illustrate the versatility of Scott-Heron's poetic and musical genius. "A Legend in His Own Mind," found on *Real Eyes* (1980), exemplifies my last category — the satirical lyric. The melody consists of a slow-upbeat rhythm that features horns, bass, and cymbals. In this song Scott-Heron's voice has a deepness much like Lou Rawls'. However, his poetic, vituperative humor keeps us mindful of his role as political activist and interpreter of the evils that beset the Black community. "A Legend in His Own Mind" is a satirical portrait and story of the Black macho man. Again the title highlights content. The macho man is a legend within his own self. He is notable only to himself and only he tells the story of his exploits. In other words, he lives inside his own head. Seeing himself as "God's gift to women," the macho man brags of his exploits with women from "Canada to Mexico." "He has had more romances than L.A.'s got stars/He has had more romances than Detroit's got cars." In these lines Scott-Heron explores the same techniques he used in "Madison Avenue" and "Show Bizness," two satirical pieces from *Secrets* (1978): he enhances the humor of his invective through rhyme and repetition. Both these poetic techniques are characteristic of the traditional toasts and folktales of the Black culture. The macho man, like Possum Slim, represents a folk tradition in which both suffer from the ramifications of a slave society. Because of the aura he creates around himself, the macho man is recognizable on sight: "You hate to see him coming when you're grooving at your bar/He's the death of the party and a self-proclaimed superstar." In other words, he is an egotistical bore to the people who know him well before he speaks. Two lines from the last stanza exemplify Scott-Heron's use of poetic analogies to incite humor: "He has had more romances than airplanes got gauges/ He has had more romances than phone books got pages." Like in "Delta Man" (*Bridges*) and "Train from Washington" (*RealEyes*), Scott-Heron writes here from his knowledge of Black history and culture.

Although the categories into which I divide Gil Scott-Heron's works might seem factitious to some, they provide ample means of discussing the works of an extremely versatile and ingenious creative artist. His canon illuminates a philosophy of life that holds human affection as well as artistic and political responsibility as the underlying factors which inspire his work. This strong sense of responsibility to Black culture is rooted in his strong sense of self. Works like "A Legend in His Own Mind," "Possum Slim," "Bicentennial Blues" and "Shah Mot" unmask a self-esteem that finds its source in his knowledge of his past, Black people's past, and his relationship to this past. If he seems to move us to violence at times, we can attribute this feeling to the power of his words, the quality of his voice, and the shaping of his poetic craft. In discussing the Black artist, Neal asserts that this sense of violence is a necessary link in the bond between the artist and his audience:

For the first violence will be internal — the destruction
of a weak spiritual self for a more perfect self. But
it will be a necessary violence. It is the only thing
that will destroy the double-consciousness — the tension
that is in the souls of Black folk.[7]

The songs on *Reflections* (1981) and *Moving Target* (1982) continue Scott-Heron's commitment to awakening Black minds to the political malaise that impedes the "destruction of a weak spiritual self" and, consequently, that exacerbate the "tension that is in the souls of Black folk." The song/poem "B Movie," along with "The Bottle" and "The Revolution Will Not Be Televised," have become the poet's paradigm for the manipulative, exploitative, and tranquilizing embodiments of capitalism. The entire Western hemisphere is a "B Movie" in which the United States plays the leading role by staging events all aimed at capitalistic gain. Quite similar to the much earlier "The Revolution Will Not Be Televised," "B Movie" progresses through a catalogue of political figures, movie stars, television figures, entertainers who play roles in setting the psychological and economical trends that shape Western culture. These two poems and their companion piece "Re-Ron" are timeless poetic collages that address the extent of the United States' orchestrated corruption from Lebanon to El Salvador, from Libya to Grenada.

Another salient characteristic of Scott-Heron's poetry is its timelessness. A prophet well in tune with the rhythms of Black lives, Scott-Heron, since the 1970's, has presaged most, if not all, of the major problems that beset contemporary Black and mainstream American society. The poems in this collection from "Coming From A Broken Home," the "Movie" poems, "Winter in America," "Johannesburg," "Pieces of A Man," "Small Talk at 125th and Lenox," "Paint It Black," to "A Poem For Jose Campus Torres" all demonstrate that Black homes with single parents, capitalistic greed, apartheid, Black urban life, and racism are no different in 1990 than they were in the early 1970's when many had hoped for change. The killing of poet and novelist Henry Dumas in 1968 in a subway station in New York is no different from the situation Scott-Heron describes in "What You See Ain't What You Goetz," a poem based on Bernard Goetz' murder and shooting of young Black male teenagers in a New York City subway.

The same forces that acquitted Bernard Goetz manifest in "Space Shuttle" and "Whitey On The Moon." Making the connection between Wall Street (capitalism), defense programs, the destruction of the ozone layer, and space exploration, "Space Shuttle" attacks the hypocrisy embodied in space exploration programs that ignore poverty, homelessness, social discontent, as well as the marked changes in the weather. The two poems make excellent companion pieces, for while "Space Shuttle" focuses com-

81

prehensively on the ludicrousness of taking the arms race into space, our fears about the changes in the atmosphere, Reagan's (Ray-gun) role in escalating space exploration, and the wasted billions spent on obsolete missiles, "Whitey On The Moon" sardonically treats the effect of this waste felt by those Blacks who make up the grass roots. The poem progresses through a set of rhymed couplets interrupted by a slight variation on the phrase "Whitey on the moon:"

A rat done bit my sister Nell.
(with Whitey on the moon)
Her face and arms began to swell.

Each "three-line couplet" emerges as a metaphor that humorously illustrates that the money spent in space exploration belongs to the American Black masses.

The unique style of "Whitey On The Moon," like all of Scott-Heron's poetry, challenges Western aesthetic standards. Embodied in this challenge are the reasons why it is important not only that we hear Scott-Heron's messages, but also that we see them in printed form. *So Far, So Good* allows those skeptics who believe that music camouflages bad poetry to experience Scott-Heron's poetic innovations and precision. In other words, this important collection of poetry defies the notion of those who might hold that Scott-Heron is more musician than he is poet. He is indeed both priest and griot, making juju with the word on his people. Representing twenty years of political and spiritual commitment, stylistic virtuosity, and thematic diversity, the poems collected here address political hypocrisy (the "Movie" poems," "Winter in America," "The Revolution Will Not Be Televised," "Bicentennial Blues," "H2O Gate Blues," and "The Ghetto Code"); alcoholism ("The Bottle"); apartheid ("Johannesburg"); the deteriorating effect of racism on Black psyches and the need for self-revitalization and healing ("Pieces Of A Man," "Lady Day and John Coltrane," "I Think I'll Call It Morning," and "The Vulture"); and catalogue the daily realities of Black life ("Small Talk At 125th and Lenox" and "Paint It Black") as well as the personal, mellow lyrics ("Coming From A Broken Home" and "The Oldest Reason In The World").

At the end of "The World," Scott-Heron repeats the earlier message of "Song of the Wind": he reiterates the importance of getting the word to the people. He says that we can change the world and that we must believe that we can change the world. The publication of *So Far, So Good* is a demonstration of the power of the word and of the people's need for that power.

Works cited

Neal, Larry. "And Shine Swam On." *Black Fire: An Anthology of Afro-American Writing*. Ed. by LeRoi Jones and Larry Neal. New York: William Morrow, 1968.

Discography / Bibliography

Publications

(1) *The Vulture* (novel) 1970, World Publishing
(2) *Small Talk at 125th & Lenox* (poetry) 1970, World Publishing
(3) *The Nigger Factory*, novel (1972) The Dial Press
(4) *The Mind of Gil Scott-Heron* (poetry booklet/LP), 1979,
　　Arista

Recordings

(1) *Small Talk at 125th & Lenox*, 1970, Flying Dutchman Records
(2) *Pieces of a Man*, 1971, Flying Dutchman
(3) *Free Will*, 1972, Flying Dutchman
(4) *Winter In America*, 1974, Strata-East
(5) *The Revolution Will Not Be Televised* (compilation), 1974,
　　Flying Dutchman
(6) *First Minute of a New Day*, 1975, Arista
(7) *From South Africa to South Carolina*, 1975, Arista
(8) *It's Your World*, 1976, Live Double LP set, Arista
(9) *Bridges*, 1977, Arista
(10) *Secrets*, 1978, Arista
(11) *The Mind of Gil Scott-Heron*, 1979, Arista
(12) *1980*, 1980, Arista
(13) *Real Eyes*, 1980, Arista
(14) *Reflections*, 1981, Arista
(15) *Moving Target*, 1982, Arista
(16) *The Best of Gil Scott-Heron*, 1984, Arista

Appearances as Guest Artist

(1) No Nukes, Musicians United for Safe Energy, 1980, Electoral/ Asylum
(2) Sun City, Artists Against Apartheid, 1985, Manhattan

Films/Videos

(1) *The Best of Saturday Night Live*, Host: Richard Pryor, NBC
(2) *No Nukes*, 1980, produced by MUSE (Musicians United for Safe Energy), Warner Bros., LP available on Electra-Asylum
(3) *Black Wax*, 1983, produced by Independent Television (ITV), London, United Kingdom and Mug-Shot Productions, Sony Video
(4) *Cool Running*, 1984, produced by Reggae Sunsplash, Sony Video scheduled October, 1988 release
(5) *A Matter of Struggle*, produced by New Line Cinema w/Richie Havens, 1986